# DALLAS COWBOYS

BY JOSH ANDERSON

**Stride**
An Imprint of The Child's World®
childsworld.com

**Published by The Child's World®**
800-599-READ • www.childsworld.com

**Copyright © 2023 by The Child's World®**
All rights reserved. No part of this book
may be reproduced or utilized in any form
of by any means without written permission
from the publisher.

**Photography Credits**
Cover: © Julio Aguilar / Stringer / Getty Images; page 1: © Africa Studio / Shutterstock; page 3: © Ronald Martinez / Staff / Getty Images; page 5: © Tom Pennington / Staff / Getty Images; page 6: © Michael Ochs Archives / Handout / Getty Images; page 9: © Ronald Martinez / Staff / Getty Images; page 10: © Tom Pennington / Stringer / Getty Images; page 11: © stevezmina1 / Getty Images; page 12: © Ronald Martinez / Staff / Getty Images; page 12: © Elsa / Staff / Getty Images; page 13: © Icon SMI / Newscom; page 13: © Tom Pennington / Stringer / Getty Images; page 14: © Tom Pennington / Staff / Getty Images; page 15: © Ronald Martinez / Staff / Getty Images; page 16: © Al Bello / Staff / Getty Images; page 16: © DAVID GREENE / "Ai Wire Photo Service" / Newscom; page 17: © MBR-Ai Wire / "Ai Wire Photo Service" / Newscom; page 17: © Ronald Martinez / Staff / Getty Images; page 18: © Ronald Martinez / Staff / Getty Images; page 18: © Tony Tomsic / SportsChrome / Newscom; page 19: © Al Bello / Staff / Getty Images; page 19: © Ronald Martinez / Staff / Getty Images; page 20: © Richard Rodriguez / Stringer / Getty Images; page 20: © Tom Pennington / Staff / Getty Images; page 21: © Patrick McDermott / Stringer / Getty Images; page 21: © Tom Pennington / Staff / Getty Images; page 22: © Rick Stewart / Stringer / Getty Images; page 23: © Lutz Bongarts / Staff / Getty Images; page 23: © stevezmina1 / Getty Images; page 25: © Stephen Dunn / Staff / Getty Images; page 26: ©  Staff / Getty Images; page 29: © Tom Pennington / Staff / Getty Images

**ISBN Information**
9781503857629 (Reinforced Library Binding)
9781503860469 (Portable Document Format)
9781503861824 (Online Multi-user eBook)
9781503863187 (Electronic Publication)

**LCCN** 2021952662

**Printed in the United States of America**

# TABLE OF CONTENTS

Go Cowboys! ............................................... 4
Becoming the Cowboys ......................... 6
By the Numbers ...................................... 8
Game Day ................................................ 10
Uniform .................................................... 12
Team Spirit .............................................. 14
Heroes of History ................................... 16
Big Days ................................................... 18
Modern-Day Marvels ............................ 20
The GOAT ................................................ 22
The Big Game ......................................... 24
Amazing Feats ....................................... 26
All-Time Best .......................................... 28

Glossary ............................................. 30
Find Out More ................................... 31
Index and About the Author .......... 32

# GO COWBOYS!

The Dallas Cowboys compete in the National Football **League's** (NFL's) National Football Conference (NFC). They play in the NFC East **division**, along with the New York Giants, Philadelphia Eagles, and Washington Commanders. Fans in Dallas have seen their team in the Big Game a lot! The Cowboys have won the **Super Bowl** five times! That's more than all but three other teams. The Cowboys are also one of the few teams to ever win the big game two years in a row! Let's learn more about the Cowboys!

## NFC EAST DIVISION

**Dallas Cowboys**

**New York Giants**

**Philadelphia Eagles**

**Washington Commanders**

TONY POLLARD (LEFT) JOINED THE COWBOYS IN 2019 AFTER A SUCCESSFUL COLLEGE CAREER AT THE UNIVERSITY OF MEMPHIS.

# BECOMING THE COWBOYS

The Cowboys joined the NFL as an **expansion team** in 1960. The team was originally going to be called the Steers, and then the Rangers. Finally, the team owners settled on Cowboys. The team struggled on the field in its first few seasons. But from 1966 to 1983, the team missed the **playoffs** only once! The team made it to the Super Bowl five times during this stretch, winning twice. Dallas had the same head coach, Tom Landry, for its first 29 seasons!

DON MEREDITH STARTED 83 GAMES AS A QUARTERBACK FOR THE COWBOYS DURING THE 1960s.

# BY THE NUMBERS

The Cowboys have won **EIGHT** NFC Championships.

**20** Cowboys enshrined in the Pro Football **Hall of Fame**

**530** points scored by the team in 2021—a Cowboys record!

**25** division titles for the Cowboys

WIDE RECEIVER TERRELL OWENS PLAYED THREE SEASONS FOR THE COWBOYS AND CAUGHT 38 TOUCHDOWN PASSES.

THE VIDEO BOARD AT AT&T STADIUM WEIGHS ROUGHLY THE SAME AS 18 FIRE TRUCKS AND HAS ITS OWN ELEVATOR SYSTEM SO TECHNICIANS CAN MAINTAIN AND REPAIR IT.

# GAME DAY

Since 2009, the Cowboys have played their home games at AT&T **Stadium**. The building is located in Arlington, Texas. On a typical game day, AT&T Stadium holds 80,000 fans, but up to 100,000 can squeeze in for a really big game! The stadium's domed roof is nearly 300 feet (91 m) tall. That makes it one of the tallest domes in the entire world. Fans who don't have seats close to the action don't have to worry, though. The video board at AT&T Stadium is larger than a regulation basketball court!

## We're Famous!

The Cowboys are so popular that even the team's cheerleaders have their own television show. *Dallas Cowboys Cheerleaders: Making the Team* has been on the CMT network for 16 seasons. The show follows the formation of the Cowboys Cheerleaders before each season as people compete to make the squad!

# UNIFORM

BLUE

WHITE

# Truly Weird

The 1967 NFL Championship game between the Cowboys and the Green Bay Packers is nicknamed "The Ice Bowl." The temperature in Green Bay, Wisconsin, during the game reached –13 degrees. The turf-heating system at Lambeau Field malfunctioned before the game. This meant that the moisture on the field turned to ice as the game wore on. The Cowboys lost the classic contest 21–17.

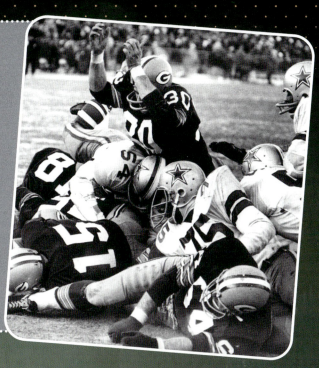

# Alternate Jersey

Sometimes teams wear an alternate jersey that is different from their home and away jerseys. It might be a bright color or have a unique theme. Every year from 2004 to 2012, the Cowboys wore their "throwback" uniforms for their Thanksgiving Day game. These uniforms were similar to the ones the team wore in their first five seasons.

ROWDY HAS BEEN CHEERING FOR THE COWBOYS SINCE 1996.

# TEAM SPIRIT

Going to a game at AT&T Stadium can be a blast. The stadium has one of largest seating capacities in the NFL. That means you could be surrounded by up to 100,000 people at a Cowboys game! The Dallas Cowboys Cheerleaders are one of the most well-known cheerleading squads in the world. They entertain fans at every home game. They're joined on the sidelines by Rowdy, the team's mascot. Rowdy is a person dressed in a cowboy costume. He sometimes enters the stadium on a four-wheeler, tossing T-shirts to fans in the crowd. Hungry fans at the stadium can enjoy the unique frankfurters at Sumo Hot Dogs.

ROWDY

# HEROES OF HISTORY

### Troy Aikman
**Quarterback | 1989–2000**

Aikman's 90 wins as a starting quarterback during the 1990s are more than any other player during that time. He led the Cowboys to three Super Bowl victories. Aikman was picked for six **Pro Bowls** and is a member of the Pro Football Hall of Fame.

### Michael Irvin
**Wide Receiver | 1988–1999**

Irvin was a key player on three Cowboys Super Bowl winning teams. His 74.9 yards receiving per game ranks 12th all-time. Irvin ranks second among all Cowboys in receiving yards (11,904) and catches (750). He is a member of the Pro Football Hall of Fame.

**Roger Staubach**
Quarterback | 1969–1979

Staubach used his skill as a passer to lead the Cowboys to their first two Super Bowl victories. He was nicknamed "Captain Comeback" for his ability to lead the Cowboys back from behind late in games. He was enshrined in the Pro Football Hall of Fame in 1985.

**DeMarcus Ware**
Linebacker | 2005–2013

Ware anchored the Cowboys defense for nearly a decade. He led the league in **sacks** in 2008 and 2010. He ranks ninth all-time with 138.5 career sacks. He also led the league in tackles for loss three times. Ware was chosen for nine Pro Bowls during his career.

**JANUARY 16, 1972**

The Cowboys defeat the Miami Dolphins in Super Bowl 6 24–3. It's the **franchise's** first win in the big game!

Quarterback Roger Staubach leads Dallas to a 27–10 victory over the Denver Broncos in Super Bowl 12.

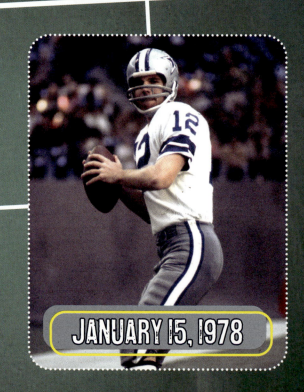

**JANUARY 15, 1978**

# BIG DAYS

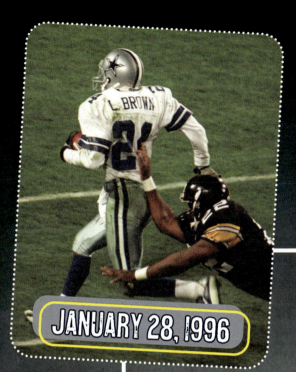

JANUARY 28, 1996

The Cowboys win their third Super Bowl in four years when they defeat the Pittsburgh Steelers 27–17.

The Cowboys win their first playoff game with Dak Prescott as their quarterback—a 24–22 victory over the Seattle Seahawks.

JANUARY 5, 2019

# MODERN-DAY MARVELS

**Trevon Diggs**
Cornerback | Debut: 2020

Diggs played his college football at the University of Alabama. In 2021, Diggs was one of the best defensive backs in the NFL. He finished with 11 interceptions. Diggs returned two of his interceptions for touchdowns. He was rewarded with his first trip Pro Bowl after the 2021 season.

**Ezekiel Elliott**
Running Back | Debut: 2016

The Cowboys selected Elliott fourth overall in the 2016 NFL Draft. He led the league in rushing yards in two of his first three seasons. He has been chosen for the Pro Bowl three times and helped lead Dallas to the playoffs three times.

## Ceedee Lamb
Wide Receiver | Debut: 2020

After starring at Oklahoma University, Lamb was the Cowboys' first-round pick in the 2020 Draft. His 74 catches in 2020 were a record for a Cowboys **rookie**. He also finished second on the team with 935 receiving yards as a rookie. In 2021, Lamb led the team with 1,102 receiving yards and earned a trip to the Pro Bowl.

## Dak Prescott
Quarterback | Debut: 2016

Prescott set an NFL rookie record by attempting 176 passes without throwing an interception to start his career. During that same season, Prescott led the Cowboys to 11-straight victories. He was chosen for the Pro Bowl in two of his first three seasons.

EMMITT SMITH'S 25 TOUCHDOWNS IN 1995 ARE THE FIFTH-MOST IN A SINGLE SEASON IN NFL HISTORY.

# THE GOAT
### GREATEST OF ALL TIME

## EMMITT SMITH

Smith is the NFL's all-time leader in rushing yards (18,355) and rushing **touchdowns** (164). He rushed for more than 1,000 yards in 11-straight seasons, leading the league in rushing yards four times. He was a key part of the Cowboys teams that won three Super Bowls from 1992 to 1995. Smith is a member of the Pro Football Hall of Fame and a member of the NFL's 100th Anniversary All-Time Team.

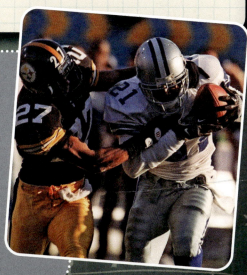

### FAN FAVORITE
**Deion Sanders–Cornerback**
1995-1999

"Prime Time" was one of the most electric players of his era. He delighted Cowboys fans with his electric speed as both a defender and punt returner. In 1998, he returned two punts for touchdowns. He was chosen for the Pro Bowl eight times—four with the Cowboys.

# THE BIG GAME

## JANUARY 31, 1993 – SUPER BOWL 27

It had been 14 seasons since the Cowboys last appeared in the Super Bowl. Coach Jimmy Johnson led the team into Super Bowl 27 against the Buffalo Bills. The game remained close into the second quarter, with Dallas leading 14–10. From there, the Cowboys offense took over. Troy Aikman threw four touchdown passes, including two to wide receiver Michael Irvin. Emmitt Smith rushed for 108 yards. By the end, Dallas had scored more points than all but one team in Super Bowl history. They finished the game with a 52–17 victory.

AFTER WINNING SUPER BOWL 27, THE COWBOYS WENT ON TO WIN TWO OUT OF THE NEXT THREE SUPER BOWLS.

TOM LANDRY LED THE COWBOYS TO 270 VICTORIES OVER 29 SEASONS.

# AMAZING FEATS

**4,903 Passing Yards** — In 2012 By **QUARTERBACK** Tony Romo

**1,845 Rushing Yards** — In 2014 By **RUNNING BACK** DeMarco Murray

**16 Receiving Touchdowns** — In 2014 for **WIDE RECEIVER** Dez Bryant

**11 Interceptions** — In 1981 for **DEFENSIVE BACK** Everson Walls

# ALL-TIME BEST

### PASSING YARDS
Tony Romo
34,183
Troy Aikman
32,942
Roger Staubach
22,700

### RUSHING YARDS
Emmitt Smith
17,162
Tony Dorsett
12,036
Ezekiel Elliott
7,386*

### RECEIVING YARDS
Jason Witten
12,977
Michael Irvin
11,904
Tony Hill
7,988

### SACKS**
DeMarcus Ware
117
Harvey Martin
114
Randy White
111

### SCORING
Emmitt Smith
986
Rafael Septien
874
Dan Bailey
834

### INTERCEPTIONS
Mel Renfro
52
Everson Walls
44
Charlie Waters
41

*as of 2021
**unofficial before 1982

TIGHT END JASON WITTEN PLAYED 16 SEASONS FOR THE COWBOYS.

# GLOSSARY

**division** (dih-VIZSH-un): a group of teams within the NFL that play each other more frequently and compete for the best record

**expansion team** (ek-SPAN-shun TEEM): a new team added to the league

**franchise** (FRAN-chyz): a professional sports team

**Hall of Fame** (HAHL of FAYM): a museum in Canton, Ohio, that honors the best players in NFL history

**league** (LEEG): an organization of sports teams that compete against each other

**playoffs** (PLAY-ahfs): a series of games after the regular season that decides which two teams play in the Super Bowl

**Pro Bowl** (PRO BOWL): the NFL's All-Star Game where the best players in the league compete

**rookie** (RUH-kee): a player playing in his first season

**sack** (SAK): when a quarterback is tackled behind the line of scrimmage before he can throw the ball

**stadium** (STAY-dee-uhm): a building with a field and seats for fans where teams play

**Super Bowl** (SOO-puhr BOWL): the championship game of the NFL, played between the winners of the AFC and the NFC

**touchdown** (TUTCH-down): a play in which the ball is brought into the other team's end zone, resulting in six points

# FIND OUT MORE

## IN THE LIBRARY

Bulgar, Beth and Mark Bechtel. *My First Book of Football.* New York, NY: Time Inc. Books, 2015.

Jacobs, Greg. *The Everything Kids' Football Book, 7th Edition.* Avon, MA: Adams Media, 2021.

Sports Illustrated Kids. *The Greatest Football Teams of All Time.* New York, NY: Time Inc. Books, 2018.

Wyner, Zach. *Dallas Cowboys.* New York, NY: AV2 Books, 2020.

## ON THE WEB

Visit our website for links about the Dallas Cowboys:
**childsworld.com/links**

Note to parents, teachers, and librarians: We routinely verify our web links to make sure they are safe and active sites. Encourage your readers to check them out!

# INDEX

Aikman, Troy 16, 24, 28
Arlington, Texas 11
AT&T Stadium 10–11, 15

Diggs, Trevon 20

Elliott, Ezekiel 20, 28

Irvin, Michael 16, 24, 28

Johnson, Jimmy 24

Lamb, Ceedee 21
Landry, Tom 7, 26

National Football Conference (NFC) 4, 8
NFL Draft 20–21

Prescott, Dak 19, 21

Romo, Tony 27–28
Rowdy 14–15

Sanders, Deion 23
Smith, Emmitt 22–24, 28
Staubach, Roger 17–18, 28
Super Bowl 4, 7, 16–19, 23–25

Ware, DeMarcus 17, 28

## ABOUT THE AUTHOR

Josh Anderson has published over 50 books for children and young adults. His two boys are the greatest joys in his life. Hobbies include coaching his sons in youth basketball, no-holds-barred games of Apples to Apples, and taking long family walks. His favorite NFL team is a secret he'll never share!